For Morgan
M.P.

For Marc
M.F.

DK Publishing, Inc.
95 Madison Avenue
New York, New York 10016

Visit us on the World Wide Web at http://www.dk.com

ISBN 0-7894-2520-3

Printed and bound in Singapore.

First American Edition, 1998
First published by Zirkoon uitgevers b.v. Amsterdam, The Netherlands 1998

2 4 6 8 10 9 7 5 3 1

SHANTI

Maartje Padt & Mylo Freeman

A DK INK BOOK • DK PUBLISHING, INC.

Shanti didn't know if she was the hungriest zebra in Africa, or the sleepiest. What she did know was that something was going to happen—happen soon.

It might be something wonderful, it might be something scary. Shanti wasn't worried. As long as the herd stayed together, they would be safe.

Then Shanti smelled lion.

The other zebras smelled lion
too. They galloped away.

The zebras ran and ran, but Shanti was too achy
and tired to keep up for very long. The lion was gone,
but the only zebra Shanti could see was her own
reflection in the water hole.

Something rustled in the thorn tree. "Who's there?" Shanti called.

"It's me," whispered the chameleon.

"Oh, Chameleon," said Shanti, "it's getting dark and I'm alone."

"Don't worry, Shanti," said Chameleon. "You won't be alone much longer."

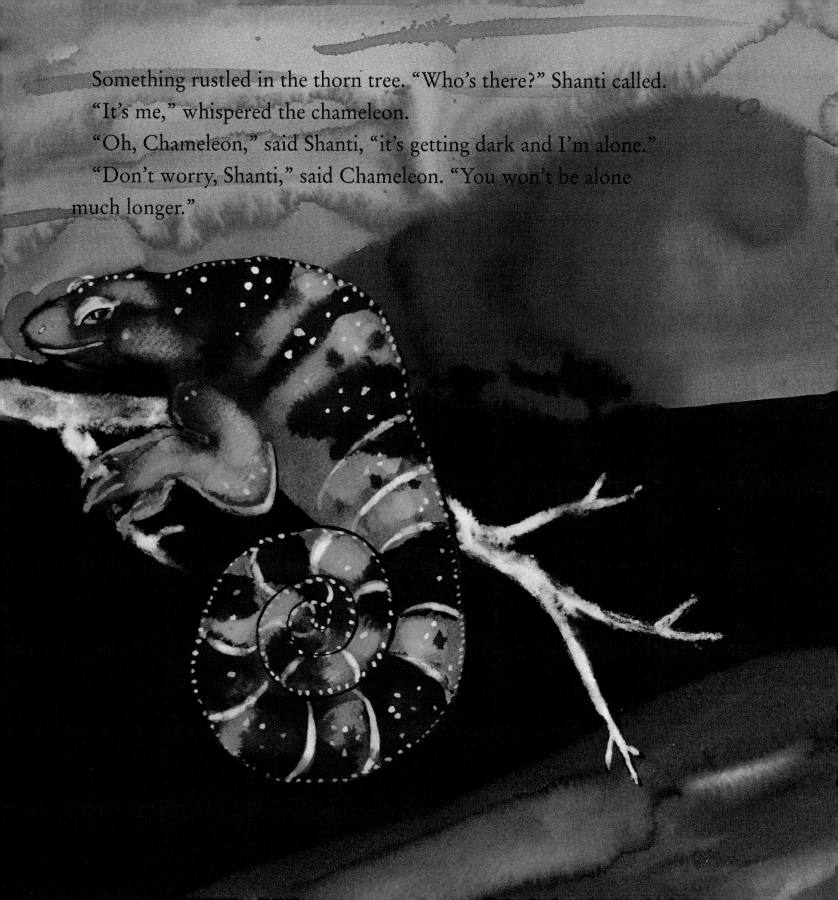

"But where are the other zebras?" asked Shanti.
"Why don't you look by the baobab trees?" said Chameleon.
So Shanti trotted over to the baobab trees. "Who's there?"
she called.

"It's us," screeched the colobus monkeys.
"Oh, monkeys," said Shanti, "I'm all alone."
"Don't worry, Shanti," said Uncle Colobus.
"You won't be alone much longer."
"But where are the other
zebras?" asked Shanti.

"Why don't you look by
the termite mounds?" said
Uncle Colobus.
So Shanti ambled over to
the termite mounds. "Who's
there?" she called.

"It's me," snorted the rhinoceros.

"Oh, Rhinoceros," said Shanti, "I'm so alone."

"Don't worry, Shanti," said Rhinoceros. "You won't be alone much longer."

"But where are the other zebras?" asked Shanti.

"Why don't you look by the edge of the forest?" said Rhinoceros.

So Shama leaned over to the edge of
the forest. "Who's there?" she called.

"It's me," hissed the viper.

"Oh, Viper," said Shanti, "I'm lost and alone."

"Don't worry, Shanti," said Viper. "You won't be alone much longer."

"But where are the other zebras?" asked Shanti.

"Why don't you look on the savanna?" said Viper.

So Shanti lumbered across the
savanna. "Who's there?" she called.

"It's us," said the impalas.

"Oh, impalas," said Shanti, "I'm tired and alone."

"Don't worry, Shanti," said Mama Impala. "You won't be alone much longer."

"But where are the other zebras?" asked Shanti.

"Why don't you look right above you?" said Mama Impala.

So Shanti looked right above her. "Who's there?" she called.

"It's me," yawned a giraffe.
"Oh, Giraffe," said Shanti, "I'm
scared and alone."
"Don't worry, Shanti," said Giraffe.
"You won't be alone much longer."
"But where are the other
zebras?" asked Shanti.
"Why don't you look by the
river?" said the giraffe.
So Shanti trudged over to
the river. "Who's there?"
she called.

"It's us," said Turtle and Crocodile. "Oh, Turtle, Crocodile," said Shanti,
"I've never felt so alone."

"Don't worry, Shanti," said Crocodile. "You won't be alone much longer."

"But where are the other zebras?" asked Shanti.

"Why don't you look in the hills?" said Turtle.

So Shanti dragged herself to the hills.
"Who's there?" she called.
"It's us," trumpeted the elephants.

"Oh, elephants," said Shanti, "I'm lost and tired and scared and alone."
"Don't worry, Shanti," said Grandmother Elephant. "You won't be alone much longer."
"But where are the other zebras?" asked Shanti.

"Why don't you just get some sleep?" said Grandmother Elephant. So Shanti got some sleep. She didn't sleep long. Something wonderful was happening—happening right now.

And as the sun dawned over mountain and river, forest and savanna, Shanti's baby was born.

Shanti wasn't scared and she wasn't
alone. She licked her colt clean and
named him Uzuri.

Uzuri was drinking his mother's milk when
the zebra herd rambled over.
"Oh, Shanti," whinnied the zebras, "we
were scared and alone without you."
"Don't worry, friends," said Shanti. "Why
don't you come and meet Uzuri?"